CADAVER DOG

Alan Horsfield

This edition published in 2017 by EJH Talent Promotion
First published in 2003 by Lothian Press

Requests and enquiries should be addressed to:
Alan Horsfield, 9 Milman Drive, Craiglie QLD 4877
anehorsfield@westnet.com.au

National Library of Australia Cataloguing-in-Publication data:

Creator:	Horsfield, Alan, author.
Title:	Cadaver dog / Alan Horsfield ; Rosemary Peers, editor ; Nancy Bevington, cover design.
ISBN:	9780648027003 (paperback)
	9780994457998 (ebook)
Target Audience:	For young adults.
Subjects:	Dogs—Juvenile fiction.
	Murder—Investigation—Juvenile fiction.
	Young adult fiction.

Proofread by Rosemary Peers
Cover design and internal graphics by Nancy Bevington
Book design, layout and production by DiZign Pty Ltd, Sydney

Printed in Australia

Contents

To the ghosts of the teachers and students that haunt the many abandoned small schools scattered throughout the Australian bush.

Chapter 1

Rocky Road Ahead

The narrow, over-patched strip of broken bitumen suddenly turned into rutted, corrugated, rocky road. The bullet-damaged road sign gave less than 50-m warning: GRAVEL SURFACE AHEAD.

'Not far now,' reassured Shane's father.

The narrow strip of broken bitumen had been, just a few kilometres back, a wider sealed roadway. Wide enough for two vehicles. It didn't last long. A bit like his parents' marriage. Maybe nowadays, Shane reflected, eighteen years was not that bad!

Shane stared through the windscreen as his father negotiated the rough surface. The potholes and gutters across the road jarred right through the suspension of the old Holden utility.

The caravan they were towing objected to the road, the sudden braking and the unexpected swerves to avoid sharp stones that seemed to have been purposely placed in the hard surface to destroy as many tyres as possible. The ute lurched and swayed. The van, like some obstinate beast, pulled and swayed in the opposite direction. It also had to tolerate the dust and stones thrown at its once clean front panel.

The main road to the mountains, with its centre line and well-graded edges, had long been left behind.

Shane's father, an ex-police driver, swore as he braked and swerved to avoid yet another pothole, the van's momentum forcing the utility to edge forward. They continued down the centre of the road. They hadn't passed another vehicle for at least half an hour.

Shane watched the passing scenery — long paddocks of yellowing grass and scraggy bushes, clumps of black ironbark trees and a scattering of small farmhouses. Many looked deserted or uncared for. Rusting vehicles were the basic garden decoration. The only sign of modern living was the occasional TV antenna that, more often than not, seemed attached to the house with a minimum of effort and thought.

A small bridge rattled and bounced as they inched across the loose planks.

'Bit like hill-billy country,' said Shane's father with a hint of a smile.

Shane didn't reply. For a brief moment his thoughts drifted to Sheryl, a girl in his class at school. He wondered what she might be doing.

He puzzled over what his mother might be doing — enjoying. He certainly wasn't doing any enjoying.

What had started out as a bit of an escape adventure was becoming a depressing journey into the unknown.

His high hopes of the morning departure were being whittled away with every kilometre they travelled. His mood was getting worse. He was scared he might be sick. The perpetual swaying, the smell of fuel, the dust that was seeping into the cabin and the heat of the sun through the windscreen didn't add to his comfort and well-being.

They edged past another bullet-battered road sign. SCHOOL. It was leaning across a broken fence that separated the roadside grass from a paddock of the same grass.

'Nearly there!' announced Shane's father. It sounded more like relief than excitement.

Along the road, sitting a few metres back from the curve, a small grey building came into view.

Shane's father dropped the ute back to second gear as they reached an opening in the fence. As his father manoeuvred the ute and the van across the gutter and into the drive, Shane observed the bent and rusted gate. It hadn't been shut for years. Its lowest bar had sunk into the ground and was overgrown with grass and small bushes.

The grey building was labelled with a peeling sign. IRONBARK RIDGE PUBLIC SCHOOL — 1887. No one had bothered to record the year it had closed.

The building was in an advanced state of decay. Windows had been roughly boarded up, the door on the back verandah hung at a dangerous angle. Boards from the steps had been removed or rotted out or eaten by white ants. Rusted guttering hung from the corners.

'That's the reason we need the caravan to start off with. Couldn't live in that!' said Shane's father as if reading Shane's thoughts.

'Not like home,' said Shane shaking his head. The afternoon shadows gave the building a foreboding grimness.

'Well, that's another story at this stage,' agreed his father with an apologetic shrug.

His father pulled up in an open area of the ground — no doubt once the play area for generations of bush kids. Now a rutted area of level, semi-barren ground.

Shane got out of the ute and surveyed the grounds. This was going to be their country place in the shadow of the mountains! The mountains were a distant border of fading blue above the scraggy foothills.

As his father uncoupled the caravan, Shane gave an involuntary shiver. He felt they were being watched by the ghosts of the ex-students of Ironbark Ridge Public School.

'We're being watched,' said Shane's father. The announcement gave Shane a small shock. He looked around quickly, not sure what to expect. He couldn't see anyone.

'Over near the fence. Just down from the school. Under the tree. It's the guy I bought the land off. Clarry Johnson. He bought it for peanuts when they closed the school.' Shane's father gave a casual wave.

Shane scanned the scrub along the fence line. Finally he saw the man. A thin runt of a man. He was standing quite still, watching, observing.

Shane joined his father behind the van and helped adjust the back van supports. He sensed they were still being silently observed.

Chapter 2

A New Day

As they sat around the embers of the campfire Shane's father had made the evening before, Shane took time to study his new environment. A restful night's sleep and some toast made over the open fire had dispelled his feelings of depression and foreboding.

Magpies were warbling their dawn song, high in the treetops.

His father, Shane noticed, was lost in thought as he sipped a steaming mug of tea.

The old schoolyard was an area of flat, degraded land that faced the road and backed onto timberland that ran down into a dry gully. On either side of the school grounds were rural properties. To the east was Clarry Johnson's property. His house, which was more like a shanty, was perched on the top of a small hill. It was surrounded by a mess of sheds and ancient trucks and vans. A thin wisp of smoke rose weakly from a corrugated-iron chimney.

A collapsing, rusting, water tank sat halfway down the hill, caught up in a dying fruit tree that was once part of a citrus orchard that spread across the hill.

Up at the house, dogs were barking angrily.

'Not our sort of farm,' said his father softly.

'It's a real mess,' agreed Shane.

'We'll turn this patch of earth into a model farm — and a new home. It'll be work for a while, but we can do it when I get settled.'

'You going to see Mum?'

'I'll give her a ring when I get to work. If I get a chance between deliveries. Got a big payroll delivery to a housing development down south. Then there's a heap of legal documents for a big trial in the city.'

Shane was silent.

'You'll be OK?' asked his father. 'I'll only be gone for the day. I'm sure you'll be all right. You can spend all day exploring our *new farm*. Tell me what you think of its potential. Don't be too critical.' He gave a soft laugh as he looked at the old school buildings. 'At least, the toilets are safe enough to use. Just!'

After his father had left for work, Shane was soon at a loose end. He wandered aimlessly around the old schoolhouse, examining the boarded building with caution.

The place was silent.

Standing on his toes he was able to peer into the gloom of the interior of the one-classroom school. He wondered where the last kids who had been taught there might have gone.

In a far corner he could just make out a bundle of material. It looked like basic bedding that might be used by a tramp sheltering from the weather.

A piece of loose corrugated iron clanged against a window frame, making Shane look about nervously.

Once more he had the distinct feeling he was being secretly watched.

The uneasy feeling stayed with him as he explored the grounds and the bush immediately behind the school, where he discovered a disused and overgrown track leading into the unknown scrub.

The morning magpies were silent. So was the bush.

Shane made his way back to the road in front of the school. A car rattled and bounced by, heading towards town, creating a cloud of dust that drifted slowly across the school grounds. To his surprise, he noticed a hut across the road, hidden in a clump of wattle and tea-tree. When he crossed the road a dog barked offensively and he caught a glimpse of someone in the doorway of the hut.

The dog went quiet.

Shane looked around nervously. Someone was coming up the road.

Shane returned to the school grounds and watched the approaching figure. To his surprise, it was female, dressed in a pink frock, and she was pushing a pram.

Unanswered questions flooded his mind. Who was she? Where was she going out here?

She got closer but seemed not to see him, even though he was standing next to an old post that had once been part of the front gate and now only supported the rusting drum that was an excuse for a mailbox.

She was young, quite young. She could have been younger than he was. Probably younger than Sheryl, he thought, then wondered why he had made the comparison.

And she was singing, softly singing, as if to calm a child that was in the old-fashioned cane pram.

As she drew level Shane smiled awkwardly, self-consciously. She didn't turn to look at him until he nodded tentatively. She stopped and studied him inquisitively.

'Are you the new teacher?' she asked respectfully, softly.

Shane shook his head, not comprehending.

'We haven't had a teacher since Mr Cullen left. He was nice. I wonder where he is now.'

'I'm no teacher,' said Shane, with a weak laugh. He didn't want to be a teacher. He wouldn't mind being a detective, but that prospect seemed to be slipping away.

She smiled brightly at him. 'Doesn't matter. But we should get a new teacher before the baby is much older. Should have a school to go to.'

She looked in the pram, smiled and began singing again.

'Want to see her?' she asked. 'I have to take her for a walk every day.'

Shane wasn't sure he did. There was something uncanny about the whole situation. He walked cautiously to the middle of the road, unsure of how to act.

'It's all right,' she said, 'she won't bite. Say hallo. Her name is Linda.'

Shane stepped closer, and looked under the large hood. His mouth went dry. The baby was a large, old-fashioned, plastic doll. Its blue eyes opened and closed as the pram was gently rocked.

'She's such a good baby. It's a pity you're not a teacher. My father said she is very bright.'

Shane's mind was racing but he was unable to react. He remained bent over the pram, trying to make sense of his situation. I'm going mad, he thought.

As he straightened up, searching for words, she said, 'Must hurry on, can't be all day.'

She started singing again as she pushed the pram down the centre of the road, leaving Shane staring after her.

It took him a moment to realise how ridiculous he must look, standing in the middle of a road, out in the bush, watching a rather simple young girl pushing a doll in a pram to some unknown destination.

He looked around guiltily. Nothing else moved. Again he had the unnerving feeling of being watched.

He glanced at the house across from the school. Nothing moved. No dogs barked.

He hurried back to the school grounds, glad to return to the dubious security they provided. He still sensed he was being watched. He cast his eyes to the caravan, half expecting to see someone waiting there.

He made his way past the back verandah and onto a large slab of rough concrete. It seemed out of place in the basic, almost primitive, school grounds. It was too small for an assembly area, even for a one-teacher school. Shane couldn't imagine it being used for any game or sport.

His father would say there was a reason for everything — a motive, however obscure. Once a policeman, always a policeman, Shane thought. But Shane could not imagine why such a slab of concrete existed.

He looked for clues but could see nothing that helped.

And the sense of not being alone lingered. Shane scanned the bush. Nothing. He scanned Clarry Johnson's hilltop. Nothing. His eyes wandered down, over the neglected orchard. Nothing.

Then, as he was about to turn away, he caught sight of someone standing perfectly still, near a half-dead fruit tree. He was sure it was Clarry. Clarry was watching him, silently watching him.

He stared in Clarry's direction. It was like watching a distant scarecrow. Still, he didn't move, but Shane had the distinct feeling that he was slowly edging behind the tree. But still watching.

He became aware of the girl's plaintive singing getting closer. He could just make the sounds of the pram coming down the gravelly road.

He quickly turned to see her come out from behind the school. She didn't look at him as she passed.

When he turned back to check on Clarry, he wasn't there. It was as if he had never existed.

Chapter 3
Second Night

For the second night, they had a campfire meal. Shane found the flames relaxing but he was vaguely troubled.

'What do you know about old Clarry, Dad?'

'*Old* Clarry? Well, let's see. Not much, I guess. His family, and most of his relatives, have been out here since the First Fleet, I'd reckon. Living off the land — just. I'd call him a bit of a hillbilly. But not to his face.'

Shane's father paused for a moment and stirred the coals with a stick before continuing. 'Bit like me, I guess.'

Shane looked at his father. He could see no comparison.

His father laughed. 'I don't mean he looks like me. We're similar. Both separated. No, that's not quite right. I'm separated. His wife disappeared. Up and left, so he said. That's when he decided to sell the block. Didn't seem much point in keeping it. The real estate agent reckons it was because he couldn't pay the rates. Not many takers for a small parcel of land out here. But the suburbs are on the move. Ten years, twenty years, and this will be prime real estate.'

The image of the girl with the pram still confused Shane but he didn't feel comfortable telling his father about her. There was something odd about her that he didn't understand. It was all too bizarre.

Silence. Bush silence.

Shane looked up at the stars through the high boughs of the ironbarks.

'Ten years' time,' his father said slowly, '*they* won't be so bright. Bet your life there will be more houses, more hobby farms, more cars, even streetlights out here — and fewer stars. But right now it's peaceful. And right now I need peace.'

Shane slept restlessly that night, the sounds of the bush more intrusive, more alien. He was sure he could hear movement around the van.

Next morning when he told his father, he said it was probably possums — or wallabies. It made sense, with so much bush about. He might even see a wallaby.

As his father climbed into the ute to leave, his mobile phone rang. Shane watched from the door of the van. He could see his father tapping the steering wheel as he listened.

As soon as the call was completed Shane's father walked back to the van. 'Change of plans,' he said.

Shane waited.

'Have to go down the coast. Might be back late. Very late. In fact, might not be back until tomorrow. Reckon you'll be OK?'

Shane thought for a moment. There was an ache in the pit of his stomach. 'Sure, Dad. I *am* almost seventeen!'

Shane's father looked at him for a moment. 'Sorry, son, can't be helped. Things are difficult but we'll get over this patch.'

Shane's jaw was locked shut.

His father continued, 'Don't worry too much. You're safer here than in the centre of Sydney. Old Clarry's all right. I should have introduced you to him. If you see him, introduce yourself. Break down the barriers. Must fly. Take care.'

And with that Shane's father patted him on the shoulder and headed for the ute. Shane forced a smile.

The ute disappeared out the gate and soon all that remained was a cloud of settling dust and the warble of a few late-morning magpies.

The dogs on the hill started barking, as if straining to get off their leashes.

Chapter 4
Strange Finds

A wave of loneliness swept over Shane as soon as his father drove off. He knew no one at Ironbark Ridge. The bush looked uninviting. His father had taken the mobile phone to work and he had no contact with the real world.

The radio, in the van, was on batteries until his father returned home to hook the car's power up to the van. Batteries didn't last forever.

The last shop he had seen was kilometres way. It was no more than a bush garage and grocery store sitting at one of the small crossroads they had passed on their way to their new farm. He couldn't remember the last person he'd seen about his age, until he remembered the girl with the pram.

No one to talk to. Well, there is the girl with the pram, he thought with a wry smile.

And he wasn't the type to sit down and read all day. He wasn't sure how long his few Christmas-present books might have to last. He was not really in a reading mood.

He wandered around the van, hoping he might be distracted by some exciting discovery.

No such luck, but he remembered the overgrown track that disappeared into the bush behind the van.

Picking up a stick, he made an instant decision to follow the track and do some bush exploring.

The track dropped gently from the ridge, winding round clumps of trees and sawn-off stumps. In places, he had to scramble over fallen trees and through tangles of broken branches. At times the track disappeared and it was a while before he picked it up again.

In the distance he heard a truck labouring along the road that followed the ridge back to civilisation.

Shane noticed that the bush was changing. The tall straight ironbarks had given way to stunted, white, scribbly gums. Large outcrops of weathered sandstone protruded from the sloping ground.

Then the track seemed to peter out altogether.

Shane was undecided as to whether he should continue down into the gully or simply retrace his steps.

Suddenly he was aware of how quiet the bush was. It was an uncanny quiet.

The fleeting thought of seeing a wallaby crossed his mind. It didn't look like wallaby country — whatever that was. He looked around nervously, not sure what he expected to see.

Nothing moved. The stunted, white-barked gums looked strangely ominous. Dead branches, like bony fingers and arms, reached to the sky for help that would not come. Growth abnormalities on the trunks looked like the distorted faces of deformed gargoyles. Bushfire burns were drying, bloody scars on a pale skin.

Shane was getting nervous. He knew he was being irrational.

In a spur of the moment decision, he threw his stick into the scrub. It tumbled through the air before smashing into a small clump of scrubby bushes. It was then he saw a large disc, maybe fifty centimetres across, nailed to the trunk of a tree.

Curious, he investigated, almost tripping over a rough spread of sandstone rocks partially hidden under a carpet of dead leaves and small branches.

On approaching the tree he saw that the rusting disc was probably the top of an old paint drum. Its purpose was obvious. Target practice. It was damaged with a dozen or so bullet holes. They formed a crude cross of perforations. They had no significance for Shane — at that point.

Finding some comfort in evidence of other human activity, Shane made his way back up the track to the van, unaware that his relaxed mood would soon come to an end.

Chapter 5

Who's Watching?

Shane saw the white caravan through the bush sooner than he expected. A return trip always seemed shorter than an outward trip. But as he came to the edge of the clearing he paused, just to reassure himself that nothing had changed since his departure.

The van site was quiet. Nothing had changed, except that the sun was a little higher in the sky.

Shane went into the van and poured himself a drink from some cold water stored in the little gas fridge. He looked across the grounds towards the lonely road through the narrow window above the little sink. Nothing stirred.

Then, just as he was putting his empty glass upside down on the draining board, he saw movement on the road. For some reason it gave him a start. As the girl with the pram emerged from behind the ramshackle school building he felt like a peeping Tom, watching from some secret place. Not willing to be seen. Embarrassed, but not sure why.

He couldn't hear her but he could see she was singing to the doll as she wheeled it along the stony road.

Weird, he thought.

He left the van, feeling uneasy. He put it down to being bored. Dad's idea of living a stress-free life in the bush wasn't quite coming up to expectations.

He wondered what his mother might be doing. She'd be in a new home — not in a caravan parked out on the edge of civilisation.

What were his schoolfriends doing? Ex-schoolfriends. Lazing on some beach, he thought, with a pang of anger and regret. Then he remembered Sheryl had said her family were going to a resort in Thailand for a holiday. More exciting than Ironbark Ridge!

His aimless wanderings ended up back on the small slab of concrete behind the schoolhouse. Sitting in the middle of the slab he again considered its purpose. Its importance to the little school. It *was* too small for any game he could think of. Except hopscotch, maybe. He didn't think primary kids played hopscotch nowadays. Except on television commercials.

Trouble was, he reckoned, the concrete looked as if it had been put down since the school had closed. Shane played listlessly with his thoughts. He should make some notes — as his father used to do. Keep a record of details as they came to mind.

His father had said mysteries were like puzzles, jigsaw puzzles. You just needed the bits in the right place and then there was no mystery.

His eyes wandered over his surroundings. The road was deserted. There were a few head of motionless cattle in the adjacent paddock. The bush behind the van now looked uninviting.

Shane turned his head to look at the Johnson property. There was no movement around the shack on top of the hill. No dogs barked. No farm animal noises.

But something was out of place.

The scraggy trees and bushes along the fence line between the school and the Johnson farm were unmoving. Then, as he stared vacantly at the scene, he had the impression of some slight movement. It was ever so slight. His first thought was to dismiss it as a breeze through the sparse leaves.

There was no breeze. Even the tall bush grass was unswaying. The summer day was warm and still.

Maybe, he reflected, it was a bird among the branches. Or even a goanna climbing the tree. It looked like goanna country.

He watched until the scene began to swim before his eyes. The effect was mesmerising. He had to blink to find focus. Maybe the sun was making him hallucinate.

Still, nothing moved. But a cold shiver ran down Shane's back.

He stood up, shaking off the feeling.

Then he heard a dog growl menacingly nearby. The hairs on the back of his neck prickled.

Slowly, he turned towards the nearby dividing fence.

The dog growled again and then barked.

And Clarry moved from the protection of his camouflaged position into a space between two dead saplings. Sentinels posted with makeshift rifles pointing skywards.

And Shane wondered just how long he had been under secret surveillance.

Chapter 6
Clarry Johnson

Clarry waved casually

It took Shane a moment to respond. And when he did wave he felt silly, that his action was awkward. It took another moment to realise that Clarry was waiting for him to meet him at the fence. He made his way through the clumps of wiry grass. His self-introduction was clumsy, self-conscious, but Clarry seemed not to notice.

The blue cattle dog sat by Clarry's feet, quietly growling at Shane's every movement until Clarry gave a rough command. The dog cowered but was not submissive.

'Don't worry about Blue. Once he gets to know you he'll probably ignore you. He's a bit suspicious, at first, about strangers.' Clarry spoke slowly, but his speech was not a drawl.

'Should get myself a dog,' said Shane.

'Don't have a dog? Yeah, should get yerself a dog. Never know when you might need one. Around here. Often get strangers on the road. Can't trust strangers.'

'Seems pretty quiet to me,' said Shane, trying hard to make his comment not sound like a criticism.

Clarry rested his hand on top of a leaning fence post. The dog settled down on its belly and panted, open-mouthed, at the rusting fence netting.

'Didn't want to sell the old school block. But things happen. Needed the money.'

Clarry rambled on. Shane only half listened to Clarry's tale of woe. He waited awkwardly.

Clarry was a thin man. He hadn't shaved for several days, maybe a week, and his hair was unkempt. Strands hung out from under his battered hat. The hat looked as if it rarely left his head.

'When the wife left … Didn't really have much enthusiasm for making the farm bigger.' He paused. 'Guess she's not really my wife any more.'

Clarry paused again.

'Did you get a divorce?' Shane asked, suddenly aware that he hadn't really been listening.

'Nah, didn't bother. I ain't going to pay good money for a settlement.'

'Then you're not really divorced?' Shane prompted.

'Nah, I guess you're right. But I ain't heard from her for years.'

'She might be dead.' Shane spoke without thinking.

Clarry looked at him, momentarily annoyed, suspicious. Then he smiled. 'Reckon, if you're right that is, then I am divorced. Weren't much good feeling between us when … when she finally left. For good. She won't be back!' he said contemptuously.

'If she's dead, then you're still not divorced. You're just widowed.'

'Don't matter what it is. She's gone. Left us to look after ourselves! Isn't right. Wasn't right!' Clarry was getting worked up.

Shane closed his lips tightly. He gazed at the old orchard, afraid he might have upset Clarry.

The dog growled and looked up at Clarry, then at Shane.

Clarry scraped at his teeth with his fingernail. 'Damn woman. Deserves whatever she gets.'

Shane wanted to return to the van. He had no conversation left.

Silence. Uncomfortable, strained silence.

'When's your father going to start doing something with the block?'

'Don't know. Think he wants to knock the old school down first.'

'Should've been knocked down years ago. I'd put a fire through it, if it was still mine. Place for tramps and hippies to hang out in. Don't want none of them wandering around the place. Don't know what they'll take. Or what other mischief they'll get up to.' Shane was surprised by the barely suppressed anger and contempt in Clarry's voice.

Clarry looked at Shane. 'As I said, don't like strangers around here.' For a moment Shane wondered if he was considered a stranger.

It was time to change the subject. 'Dad said he might put in some grapes. And olives.' Shane ran out of words for a moment. He suddenly added, 'Have to get rid of the concrete slab in the middle of the yard.'

Clarry looked at him suspiciously. 'I put that there!' But to Shane, Clarry seemed to be preoccupied with other concerns. 'Was going to be a shed,' he quickly explained.

That solves that mystery. Pretty small shed though, Shane thought, then wondered if Clarry Johnson was some sort of weirdo.

A red car laboured up the track from the road to Clarry's house on the hill. Clarry turned and watched for a moment before speaking to his dog. 'Get him, Blue!' he said with some satisfaction.

The dog stood, turned towards the track, ears pricked. Without another command it raced through the tangle of scrub and grass towards the shack.

'He ain't a stranger but I don't want him hanging around. Ellie don't want him around either.' Clarry was watching the dog race up the hill. The car had disappeared behind the outbuildings near the shack.

He turned back to Shane. 'You've seen my Ellie. She's been up and down the road a couple of times.'

Suddenly Shane was glad he hadn't made any comments about the strange person pushing the pram. It could have been embarrassing. Really embarrassing.

'She used to be all right,' Clarry went on vaguely. 'Then young Eddie Roach turned up. Cockroach I call him.'

Shane had no comment. He didn't want to get involved in Clarry Johnson's problems. He was feeling uncomfortable.

'He didn't stay around too long. Long enough, though. Too long, some might say. Including me.'

The dog, barking threateningly, had almost reached the top of the hill.

'I gotta look after Ellie. Without help. Wouldn't want anything else to happen to her.' He was looking at Shane from under his hat. His voice was quiet, but his eyes were cold, menacing.

Shane nodded in agreement, not understanding the tone in Clarry's voice.

A car horn sounded from the top of the hill and a moment later the red car could be seen winding its way down the track, working its way around the ruts, gutters and potholes. The dog barked noisily at its back wheels.

'I'd better go,' said Shane, feigning he had just remembered something. 'Dad won't be too happy with me if the van's full of dust. Or I've used up all the water before tomorrow night.'

He immediately regretted his words.

Clarry looked at him. 'He don't come home every night?' he asked slowly.

Shane shrugged.

The red car turned off the track and onto the road. As it passed by the school Clarry gave a generous wave.

The driver looked straight ahead.

Clarry sniggered and walked back towards his house.

Chapter 7
A Long Night

As night approached, a feeling of dread filled Shane's being.

As the sun sank, so did his feelings.

By six o'clock Shane's father hadn't returned to the van. If he was going to be coming home, then he would have been home some time after five-thirty. Shane found he was checking his watch every few minutes.

Clarry had left him feeling somewhat perturbed. There was something about Clarry he didn't find attractive. And it wasn't because he was a bit of an uneducated bushie.

He didn't like Clarry's dog, Blue, either.

By sunset Shane accepted that he would be spending the night alone. He felt angry with his father. And somewhere, deep inside, resentful of his mother.

When dark began to descend he locked himself in the van and lit the gas lamp. When the van wasn't hitched up to the ute, he had to save the van's power for special times. He heated some baked beans on the gas burners and ate them from the saucepan. Tried to find something to listen to on the radio.

The quiet and the dark outside the van were oppressive. Occasional bush noises added to his sense of isolation.

A small truck worked its way down the road. From the van window he watched its lights pick up shadowy trees and fence posts leaning at grotesque angles.

A momentary dim glow seemed to come from the inside of the darkened school building as the truck passed by. After a moment's surprise, Shane guessed it was the headlights of the passing truck shining through gaps in the building.

The dogs on the hill had a barking fit.

Shane was aware that he was getting nervous. He switched on the van's electric lights and turned off the heavy gas lamp. He climbed into his bed in a space at the front of the van, above the collapsible table. His father had claimed the bed at the back of the van. Jokingly, he had said he wasn't up to climbing a ladder to get into bed every night. Suited Shane. He decided to look at one of his dad's trucking magazines. It would take his mind off his loneliness — and, hopefully, help him get to sleep.

A slight breeze rustled through the trees.

Something rattled and scraped on the old school building.

A night bird gave a lonely cry.

The dogs on the hill had another barking fit.

Shane dropped his magazine and switched off the dim light. He was amazed how black night was in the bush.

Something crashed to the ground in the nearby bush.

He rolled over onto his stomach, slid open the little window at the head of the bed and peered into the dark. He could see the feeble lights of Clarry's place. They looked distant, across a silent sea of darkness.

He wondered if there were ghosts in the bush. Or even wallabies.

He wasn't feeling as brave as he had earlier in the day — when the sun was shining and he knew what all the noises were.

As his eyes became accustomed to the dark he could make out the silhouettes of nearby objects. Trees, bushes and the old school building.

It gave him a scare when he thought he saw a small, dim red glow in the old building. It disappeared as fast as it had appeared. Shane could not be sure he had seen it or whether it was a figment of his overactive imagination. His eyes playing tricks. He could become a nervous wreck before morning — or before midnight.

Somehow, he drifted off into shallow sleep.

Chapter 8
Noises in the Dark

Shane was not sure why he was suddenly awake.

The breeze seemed to be stronger, the noise from the disturbed trees louder.

Shane lay awake, on his back, perfectly still, straining his ears to isolate the noise that may have woken him. He could hear nothing. Nothing that should have caused him to be fearful.

A branch snapped and fell to the ground.

He was tense, alert, for a moment expecting another sound. His heart was beating fast.

Nothing.

And after a few moments he began to relax. He was angry with himself. Angry that he could so quickly become a trembling wreck.

The van rocked gently in a brief gust.

Shane wondered how long it would be before morning. He hoped he could last the night without something dreadful happening. He knew it was a foolish thought.

Another small branch crashed to the ground, somewhere near the van. The noise made him shudder.

A twig snapped. The noise seemed just outside his window.

Then came the sound of scrunching gravel. Someone's out there, walking around the van, Shane thought, horrified.

He lay perfectly still. He imagined being attacked in his bed. He had sudden doubts about having locked the van door.

Another light gust of wind shook the van.

As noiselessly as possible, he rolled over onto his stomach again and peered out into the night.

His straining ears seemed to hiss in the heavy silence.

Then came another almost silent scrunch of gravel. Or was it his imagination?

Every nerve in Shane's body was stretched to breaking point as his eyes tried to penetrate the darkness.

He could see nothing at ground level. It was pitch black. It would almost be a relief if there was something out there, he thought.

Icy stars twinkled in a silent sky.

The breeze picked up again.

Then he froze. Terrified.

Clearly he had heard it. There was no mistake. Three melancholy, rising notes in a minor key. It was as if someone, with a warped sense of humour, had played three notes, and only three notes, on pan-pipes.

Shane rolled onto his back and lay as stiff and as taut as stretched fencing wire. But he trembled all over. His mouth was dry.

The breeze got stronger, filling the bush with new sounds, more familiar sounds. Shane waited for a repeat of the sad notes.

Slowly, his body relaxed but his imagination raced. He remembered all the terrible and gruesome things he had seen on television. Murders, assassinations, torture, explosions and horrific accidents. Once, they had happened to other people. Now, it seemed they could happen to him.

He was tempted to flee the van. Only the irrational fear that he might run straight into the arms of some deranged murderer stopped him.

The breeze eased.

Then he heard it again. The three sorrowful notes. Rising then falling. It was just outside the van. Somewhere, just on the other side of the wall where the sink and stove were located.

Shane let out a silent, involuntary scream. He thought he was about to die.

Chapter 9
Shane Investigates

Shane was not sure how he survived the trauma of the long night. He slept fitfully, only drifting off to sleep when he could no longer keep his heavy eyes open. But it was a shallow, troubled sleep and at the slightest night noise he was awake, disoriented and tense.

When dawn finally forced the ogres of the night to retreat, Shane was able to sleep for an hour or so. But he woke tired and listless. And although the terrors of the night were less real the memory of them tormented his thoughts.

The alien noises of night did not match up with the recognisable noises of day. When he explored the grounds around the van, Shane began to wonder if he had been foolish. He felt like some bumbling detective looking for non-existent clues.

There were no signs of the pan-piper. There were no sticks or twigs that had been obviously broken by some midnight stalker. No footprints on the hard, dry soil.

The breeze had dropped and the wisp of smoke from the Johnson shack on the hill rose almost vertically. There was something oddly comforting in the sight.

The school looked totally abandoned. Common sense told Shane that it was probably rat-infested. Full of creepy-crawlies.

Shane made himself some breakfast and sat down on the van's step to consider his position. He had a whole day to fill in. He didn't feel like exploring the bush again. And he was not the type to take a daytime nap, no matter how tired he was.

Listless, he stood up, picked up a stick, and wandered aimlessly around the ground. He ended up sitting on the edge of the concrete behind the school, scratching lines in the grey dirt.

It was then he saw it, caught up in a clump of spiky grass. At first he didn't recognise its significance, but a cigarette butt was a scary find.

The cigarette butt was fresh.

He didn't smoke.

His dad didn't smoke.

He hadn't seen Clarry smoke — but that didn't prove anything.

But he was almost certain he had seen a glow, at least once, in the old schoolhouse during his long journey through the night.

Shane toyed with the cigarette butt with his stick, rolling it over and poking at it, while he played with explanations of his experiences during the night.

He pushed himself to his feet and crept towards the school. He skirted the back steps' framework and crouched down to peer into the gloom through the broken and hanging door.

He could see nothing as he swayed back and forth trying to distinguish features of the classroom.

'Hey, boy! Shane! What you doing? Something in there, eh?' It was Clarry.

Shane straightened up and turned around, feeling both guilty and foolish. Sheepishly, he made his way to the fence where Clarry stood with his dog.

'Thought there was someone in there. Might be in there.' Shane stumbled over the words.

'Bloody hippie. Saw one on the road the other day. What's he up to?' Clarry had pressed the rusty netting to the ground with his scuffed boot and stepped into the school grounds. He headed straight for the building.

He carried an old rifle.

Blue bounded over the crumpled fence and followed Clarry eagerly.

Shane was left to follow.

Clarry sprang up onto the old back verandah. The dog yelped excitedly.

Yanking the door open, Clarry almost pulled it off its remaining hinge.

'You in there?' he bawled from the doorway, poking the barrel of the rifle at the space before entering the dusty room.

By the time Shane had climbed onto the verandah Clarry had finished his search. He stood defiantly in the doorway, gun hanging loosely.

Blue snarled quietly.

'He's been here! I knew it! Left some of his miserable gear in the corner. No one's safe with these guys around. Scum!' Clarry was almost talking to himself. Then he turned to Shane. 'Have a look for yerself! Bet yer dad'll shift him on.'

Shane obeyed and looked in from the doorway. In the corner was a neatish pile of rough bedding. A small photo was pinned to the wall.

'Bloody hobos!' called Clarry, as he jumped down from the verandah and headed back to his property. Blue followed.

Before climbing over the fence Clarry paused and turned back to Shane. 'Do something about him or you'll be sorry. Something'll go missing. Someone'll get hurt! I don't want no hippie around my place.'

Then he was off. Heading back up the hill, rifle over his shoulder.

Shane sat on the verandah's edge. He couldn't understand Clarry's obsessive hatred of strangers.

And when he thought about the events of the night before he was able to piece together some explanation.

The hippie, if that's what he was, had spent a night camped in the school. He hadn't really been a threat. He had certainly made himself scarce before Shane had begun his explorations.

Mass murderers didn't roll up their bunks — or pin photos neatly on the wall.

The facts didn't quite match up with Clarry's dislike of outsiders.

He looked up and saw movement, through the trees, along the road. For the briefest of moments he hoped it might be a familiar face. It was Ellie pushing her pram. He caught snatches of her melancholy singing as she got closer.

As she passed the school she paused and looked towards Shane. She gave a little wave before smiling lovingly at her doll and moving on.

Chapter 10
A Surprise

Shane was gathering sticks for the campfire when his dad returned home with several quick honks on the horn.

As Shane came out of the bush he was enveloped in the cloud of dust that had followed the ute in from the road. His father jumped out of the ute quickly, followed by a large German shepherd dog on a leash.

'Look at this, Shane! Isn't she a beauty?' called Shane's father.

It took Shane a moment to realise that his father had got the dog for him. He dropped his bundle of sticks and hurried to the ute. The dog sat obediently by his father's side.

'Where'd you get him … her?' asked Shane, looking from his father to the dog.

'Her. A guy I know — he knew about some that were being pensioned off.'

That didn't make much sense to Shane.

His father didn't elaborate. Instead, he said, 'She's well trained. So don't spoil her. She'll be a good companion. And give us a bit of security.'

Shane looked at his father inquiringly. His father continued, 'I'll feel better now, knowing you have Caddy.'

Shane looked at his father.

'That's her name.' His father shrugged. 'Give her a pat. Get to know her. Should take her for a walk. Let her get used to her new home. Keep her on the leash for a while though, I'd reckon. Let her have a run tomorrow, when she's more used to her new home.'

It took Shane a few minutes to realise just how the dog could change his new life. The nights of fear could be a thing of the past.

'You look pleased,' said his father.

Shane nodded.

His father gave him the lead. 'Take her for a walk now. Talk to her. Show her around. Then, I think, you could tie her up to the caravan step. She can sleep under the van. I've got a bag she can sleep on. And I bought some dog food. And her very own dog's dish. And I'll cook some sausages on the campfire for us!'

As Shane walked Caddy around the playground she sniffed at various objects. The corners of the old school. The wheels of the caravan. The post that once held the front gate. Shane casually looked in the rusty drum that was the mailbox. He was surprised to find some yellowing junk mail and a couple of recent, free local papers.

When a white van rattled past and tooted, Caddy pricked her ears and watched until it disappeared around a bend.

And when the dogs on the hill started a barking frenzy she was alert. She sat on her haunches and growled softly at the distant disturbance.

Chapter 11
Disaster at Night

'So you've had a rough day?' Shane's father said, looking up from a paper Shane had rescued from the mailbox. They were sitting around a twilight campfire eating sausages wrapped in slices of white bread and dripping butter and sauce.

'You know, I think I saw a tramp, or someone, on the road the other morning,' Shane's father added. 'Can't be sure.'

He stood up. 'I'll check it out,' he said as he made his way across the open space to the schoolhouse.

Shane watched from his seat, an old milk crate. His father sprang up onto the verandah and yanked the door open. Again it nearly came off its remaining hinge. He stood in the doorway for a moment before disappearing inside.

When he returned to his milk crate seat he rubbed his chin. 'Someone's been in there for sure. Quite recently too, I'd say.'

'That's what Clarry reckons,' said Shane.

Shane's father looked at him, then continued, 'Whoever's camped in there is probably not much of a threat. Poor coot's probably been living in there, on and off, for ages. Sort of got it set up as a halfway house. Uses it as a camp whenever he passes by. If that's what you'd call an empty bottle, a few smelly blankets and a flat pillow. And one small photo on the wall. Still, it's not what I want. I don't want him scaring my boy.'

Shane shrugged and smiled, embarrassed.

'But it's not really any of Clarry's business now,' his father went on. 'I wouldn't want *him* hanging about too much. He's just a little too … odd for my liking. Makes my skin crawl sometimes. Don't know why though. He's just a weed of a man!'

'I don't like his dog. Reckon he'd bite the first thing Clarry pointed at,' said Shane. He hesitated for a moment, then added, 'I heard music in the bush last night. Near the van.'

His father looked at him oddly. 'Better explain.'

Shane gave his account of the incident. Suddenly, it didn't seem so frightening.

'Probably night birds,' said his father.

'Birds don't go like that,' said Shane. He tried to whistle the three notes.

His father laughed. 'Not like that, that's for sure!'

'It wasn't birds. It sounded like … like a recorder. Like the ones we had in primary school.'

'Well, I'd bet my bottom dollar it wasn't our visitor. Not his scene, I'd say, from what I saw of his belongings. Can't really be sure he was sleeping over here last night, anyway.'

Shane asked, 'What about Clarry?'

His father looked at him. 'I really cannot imagine him tiptoeing around the bush playing a flute at some ridiculous hour of the night. Clarry might be a bit of a weirdo but he wouldn't do that. Sure it wasn't a dream?'

'It was no dream!'

'OK! OK! Then maybe it was a bird.'

'Birds don't make that sort of noise,' Shane asserted stubbornly.

'I believe you,' said his father as he stood up. He walked to the side of the van. He looked at the ground, then back to the schoolhouse as if gauging the distance. The ex-policeman's mind at work.

Shane watched silently.

His father studied the side of the dusty van. He ran his fingers over the vents behind the van's little fridge and pressed the kitchen window as if to test its security. He shook the van, testing its steadiness. It rocked gently on its springs.

He ran his eyes over the ground, then kicked a hole in the dirt with the toe of his boot. 'Nothing here that I can see,' he said matter-of-factly. 'Maybe Caddy could find something,' he added vaguely before dismissing the idea.

He returned to his milk crate, running his hand over Shane's head as he passed. 'We'll sort it out, son.'

Suddenly the previous night seemed distant and a little unreal. It was good to have someone else around, even if it was only his father.

'Time for some tea,' Shane's father said. 'Wash some of the dust away. I'll be the cook?'

Shane nodded.

As his father busied himself with the pot of hot water Shane began to doubt what he had heard. It did seem rather absurd. In the light of day it was a bit hard to imagine anyone would want to stumble around the bush at night playing a flute or recorder.

A tractor growled its way down the road. As it passed by the school the driver gave a friendly wave. They waved back. It all seemed so normal.

But Shane couldn't rid his mind of the nagging belief that he had heard something strange in the middle of the night.

Chapter 12
Fire in the Night

When Shane woke during the night, he was vaguely aware that he had been woken by an alien noise. The dog growling? Someone calling? As his eyes became accustomed to the light he realised that there was a faint glow coming in the window. At first he thought it was dawn. But there were no magpies warbling. There was a soft, indistinct crackling sound.

He thought he heard a muffled shout, or a cry.

Sleepily he turned over. It was then he noticed that the glow was not the steady glow of dawn but a flickering glow. It didn't make sense. When he looked out of his little window he realised why.

The school was on fire!

The dog barked.

Grotesque shadows danced in the trees.

It took him a moment to react.

'Dad! The school's burning down!' he cried out, suddenly fully awake.

He became aware of the roar of the flames as they turned from a bonfire into an inferno.

In a moment his father was blundering around the caravan. A light went on. His father was fumbling with his mobile phone and swearing impatiently.

Caddy's barking grew angry, urgent.

From then on the action became a blur.

By the time the local bushfire brigade arrived the old schoolhouse was little more than a large smouldering heap of burning timber and twisted corrugated iron.

Leaves on the nearby trees were scorched.

A nagging worry troubled Shane, as he and his father watched the firefighters complete clean-up operations. Then they all stopped and congregated near a corner of the building. They had found something.

Caddy sat on her haunches near Shane's feet. She was whining nervously.

'Steady, girl,' said Shane's father softly.

One fireman left the group and dashed for the truck. Within moments he was on the CB radio talking softly and urgently.

Then Shane realised why he was feeling uneasy. It wasn't the loss of the school — after all, it was on the 'get rid of' list. He gasped at the enormity of his realisation.

A person had died in the fire!

His father was looking at him. 'You right?'

'Dad, I think …' For a moment Shane was lost for words. Then he blurted out his fears. With a deep sinking feeling he remembered the cry he had vaguely heard when he first woke up.

Shane's father was silent for a moment. Shane could almost imagine his father's detective mind putting pieces together. Looking for bits that would fit.

Another fireman was talking on a mobile phone.

'Not good,' Shane's father finally said, and strangely added, 'No wonder Caddy's a bit agitated. Must be upsetting for her.'

Then he hurried off and spoke to the bushfire captain. More mobile phone calls.

When Shane's father wandered back he was deep in thought. 'Police will be here shortly.'

The police arrived in two cars, their blue lights flashing. There were urgent discussions with the remaining firefighters and their captain. They spoke to Shane's father. He looked relaxed and comfortable in their presence. Shane felt a pang of regret for his father.

And then two officers spoke to Shane.

He told a plain-clothes policeman and policewoman about the glows he had seen in the night, the cigarette butts he had found and the cry he thought he had heard.

The sun was rising when a large white police van arrived. In no time the smouldering remains of the school were cordoned off with chequered police tape. Men in orange overalls began an initial, cautious examination of the area.

Shane's father put his arm around Shane's shoulder. 'Not a good way to start a new life. Don't like accidents at the best of times. When they're on your own property you somehow feel involved. Even if you don't know the victim. Poor coot. Hope it was quick.'

Shane shivered as they turned and made their way back to the van.

'I think we should get a bite to eat. Way past breakfast time and I don't want to see whatever they are going to remove.'

Caddy was suddenly alert, tense.

Blue had started barking noisily.

'Steady, girl,' Shane's father commanded as both he and Shane looked towards Clarry Johnson's property.

Clarry was watching proceedings from his fence line. He didn't seem unduly concerned about the loss of the old schoolhouse.

'Let's eat,' said Shane's father resolutely. 'I don't like the type who turn up to watch disasters.'

The last fire truck departed as they made their way across the broken ground, and a police vehicle, with a Fire Investigation Squad sign on its door, crunched to a stop on the gravel verge outside the school fence. Its arrival was followed by lots of loud talking and more calls on mobile phones.

Both lost in their own private thoughts, they ignored the activity of the police, for now.

Chapter 13
Police Work

By mid-afternoon the police had left. It had been a morning of quiet activity. Samples of ash were collected. Bit and pieces were put into sealed bags. Unmarked police cars came and went. Mobile phones rang. Locals slowed down to stare with morbid curiosity as they drove past.

Shane watched from a distance. He was both fascinated and tense and spent a lot of time wandering around the school grounds, always watching the police at work.

Caddy's interest was more obvious. Shane's father tied her up to a tree, behind the van, away from direct view of the activity. She whined a little and looked unsettled. Shane felt sorry for her.

After breakfast, Shane's father tried to get some information from the officers working through the ashes and debris. They refused to speculate about what they had found — though they thought events were the result of an accident rather than foul play. But the chequered tape stayed in place.

Clarry had departed. Shane hadn't seen him leave. Shane casually wondered if he was watching, like a peeping Tom, from some hiding place.

Later, two men carried a long, black plastic bag off the site. They did it quickly, without fuss. They wore overalls, heavy-duty boots, protective gloves and face masks.

Finally, one of the plain-clothes officers came over and spoke to Shane's father. She told him that they were almost finished their investigations. It was evident that an unknown person had died in the fire and they would be making inquiries as to the identity of the deceased person. They would also be continuing their forensic investigations to determine the actual cause of death.

'My guess is that he was a tramp who had been seen around the area. Probably smoking in bed, drifted off, dropped the cigarette and ... whoof!' she said, raising her open palms to the sky.

Shane's father made a face. 'Why wouldn't he have woken up? Surely, the fire would have ... ? I mean, the fire wouldn't become a raging inferno *that* quickly?'

The officer shrugged, 'Could have been drinking. We did find some glass. Maybe he was sick? Had a heart attack? Who knows? Forensic will sort it out.'

They kept talking as they wandered around the grounds. They ended up at the tree where Caddy was tied up. The officer made a fuss of her, rubbed her head. Caddy licked her hands.

Shane joined them.

'You can let her off when we leave,' the officer said to Shane. 'I'm sure she will behave herself.'

Before the final police van drove away, a sign was fixed to the site: CRIME SCENE.

Shortly after that, Shane's father left.

'Must do some work,' he had said as he got into the dust-covered ute. He promised Shane he would be home about six. He didn't want Shane spending another night of worry. But as the ute disappeared down the road in a cloud of dust Shane felt a pang of loneliness and discontent.

The accident had left him bewildered. The sight of the school burning down in the middle of the night had been frightening. The thoroughness of the police search had been disturbing and yet fascinating. And the finding of the body and its removal had made Shane sad — although he had never met the person who had died so tragically in the fire.

The whole incident seemed unreal even though it was still very fresh in his mind. The vague recollection of the scream made him shiver.

He untied Caddy from the tree but he kept her on her leash. She jumped up and down excitedly, almost knocking Shane over.

Then she dragged him across the school grounds. She raced around the burnt-out school and sniffed at the ashes. She pulled Shane onto the road and looked up and down the dusty track. She sniffed at the spots where the police vehicles had been parked.

Caddy's excitement took Shane's thoughts off the disaster, for a while. But when she wanted to go inside the taped-off area around the school Shane was forced to restrain her.

And all his uneasiness returned. He could see the place in the ashes where the police had removed what remained of the uninvited visitor.

Chapter 14
Clarry's Opinion

Shane led Caddy away from the 'crime scene' and sat down on the slab of concrete behind the burnt-out school. It was covered in ash and soot but Shane was too preoccupied with his own thoughts to be concerned.

Caddy was not so despondent. She bounded around the perimeter of the slab, her leash wrapping around Shane.

'Hey,' he called, laughing at his predicament. He pulled the leash over his head as Caddy continued to circle around him. 'Cut it out, Caddy!' He rolled from his sitting position onto his back and looked up at the sky. I could be on the beach, he thought. I could be holidaying in Thailand too! No way!

Caddy calmed down and came over to look down at him inquisitively.

Suddenly, she was alert. She tensed, head held high.

'What's up, girl?' Shane asked.

Caddy whined. She turned and began sniffing around the edge of the concrete slab. The leash went taut, almost slipping out of Shane's loose grip.

Shane sat up. Caddy was working her way around the edge of the slab nosing at the dirt. Every few metres she would work an area intensely — back and forth, back and forth.

Caddy looked up at Shane when he pulled gently on the leash.

'What'ya found, Cad?' Shane asked her softly.

Caddy seemed to think about the question for a moment, then returned to her inspection of the gravelly dirt. She started pawing at the ground.

'Come off it, Caddy! Give it a break,' said Shane, standing up and tugging at the leash.

Caddy looked up at him expectantly but seemed reluctant to give up whatever had grabbed her interest. Walking away from the slab, Shane gave the leash a gentle pull. Caddy resisted for a moment, then obediently trailed after him.

'That's better,' complimented Shane sternly. Caddy caught up with him and trotted along at his side.

Back at the van, he undid the leash from her collar. 'Sit, girl!' he ordered.

Caddy sat, then after a moment lay down on her stomach, her tongue lapping at the dry, summer air.

'Good girl!' Shane nodded his approval and bent over to rub Caddy's head.

Suddenly Caddy raised her head, watching.

Shane stood, wary. He turned around to see what had caught Caddy's attention.

It took a moment to see Clarry standing at the fence. He beckoned Shane with a quick, impatient swing of the arm.

'Hey!' Clarry called. 'I want to talk to you.'

Shane bit his lip.

'Stay,' he said to Caddy and then tramped through the ash-speckled grass to obey Clarry's rough command.

This is the last thing I need, he thought.

Clarry was all toothy smiles but there was no smile in his eyes. Blue ferreted through the grass, nearby.

'Saw them police,' Clarry noted, as if waiting for an explanation, more information.

Shane was silent.

'What'd they tell you?' Clarry's head nodded up and down.

Shane shrugged. 'Didn't tell me anything much. Talked to my dad a bit.'

'What's he reckon?'

'About what?'

'The fire. And all that. I saw it all.'

Shane was tempted to say, 'I bet you did!'

Clarry was not to be put off. 'Looks like the cops had a body bag to me. Couldn't have been much of him left?'

Shane nodded. 'Yeah, they reckon it was probably the tramp, or whatever he was …'

'Won't be a loss,' growled Clarry. 'Don't want strangers hanging around!'

'He wasn't a real stranger! If it was him,' Shane defended. He was about to add, 'or might have been a *her*,' but he discarded the notion.

'Just because he's been hanging around a bit don't make him a local either!'

Shane shrugged. Clarry's attitude was making him feel uncomfortable.

'It don't! Mark my words. Good riddance some of us would say. Ellie don't like strangers wandering up and down the road. Scare her they do. Can't be right, can it?'

Shane was at a loss for words. He really couldn't imagine why Clarry was even interested in talking to him. He wasn't Clarry's type — whatever that would be. He didn't want to become involved. There was something depressing about Clarry's preoccupation with the subject.

Shane was saved from immediate further questions when a cream van went down the road. The driver honked. Blue growled.

'Mail car,' said Clarry matter-of-factly. 'Did you a favour. Told him you were the new people. So he'll know when to drop off mail. Might need a new mailbox.'

'Thanks,' said Shane lamely. 'Think I saw him go past the other day. Don't think we'll get much mail out here.' He felt a tinge of regret. He wasn't a writer and his friends didn't have *this* address. A familiar face would be a pleasant change.

'Never know,' shrugged Clarry.

Blue barked. Clarry turned to look at what had caught his attention, but continued speaking. 'At least you'll get the local paper. It can't be worth much. They give it away.'

Shane looked back to the van, checking on Caddy. She was gone.

Chapter 15
Caddy's Find

'Can't be far away,' Clarry said, as if to reassure Shane.

Shane looked back at Clarry expectantly.

'Wandered off into the bush, by the looks of it. Saw her ducking away just a moment ago. About when the mail van went by. Probably why Blue barked. Thinks some other dog's taking over his patch.' Clarry finished with a funny little cackle.

'She was supposed to sit,' said Shane, a little perplexed.

''Spect the bush was more interesting than sitting around waiting.' Clarry said it as if he was revealing some important fact he had just realised.

Shane had a vague ache in his stomach. He scanned the nearby bush for any sign of his new dog.

'Can't be far, like I said,' said Clarry.

Shane whistled. And waited.

Caddy didn't come bounding out of the bush.

In a moment of panic he remembered the road. She could get run over.

The road was quiet.

'Like I told you. She headed off into the bush. Near the big ironbark.'

Shane whistled again. Nothing.

Clarry seemed amused by Shane's anxiety.

'Damn!' growled Shane. He looked back at Clarry. 'What's down there?'

Clarry hunched his shoulders. 'Bush. And more bush. Become State Forest. Don't know why. Ain't much good timber on it. Ends up in scrubby gully. I ain't ever seen a log taken out of that country.'

Shane moved away from the fence. Blue was watching him. 'Caddy,' he called a little more urgently, afraid Clarry might sense his growing desperation.

Suddenly, Caddy emerged from the bush.

'Good girl,' called Shane, with a sense of relief.

'What's she got?'

Caddy hurried through the long grass to Shane. 'What'ya got, girl?' he said, bending down to take what she had in her mouth.

Clarry was suddenly interested. 'Bugger!'

When Shane looked up he saw that the colour had drained from Clarry's face.

'You right?' Shane was frightened Clarry was about to drop dead. Have a heart attack.

'Yeah. She's got a bone. Struth!' Clarry's eyes darted from the dog to the bush and back again.

Looking at him quizzically, Shane commented, 'Hey. It's only a dirty old bone. No big deal. Take it easy.'

Clarry seemed to come to his senses. He laughed nervously. 'Yeah. You're right. Don't know what I was thinking of! Stupid. Of course it's a bone. Bloody wallaby bone. Bush must be full of them. Bush *is* full of them, the truth of the matter is. Don't know what a dog'll find down there.'

He's raving, thought Shane. Hope it's not catching.

'Of course, it's a wallaby bone! Shouldn't let the dog have it. Get it off her.'

Shane looked at Clarry questioningly.

'Yeah, get it off her. Don't know what killed the wallaby. They carry all sorts of diseases. Full of worms. And parasites. Danger to livestock. Other dogs.'

It was the first Shane had heard of wallabies being dangerous. He had heard something about bats and some birds being a bit of a problem. But not wallabies.

'Take the thing off her,' Clarry almost ordered.

Shane patted Caddy and took hold of the bone. Caddy released the bone without argument. She watched Shane intently, following his actions.

'Give it to me,' said Clarry, putting his hand over the dividing fence. 'Got to burn some rubbish later. That's the best way to get rid of it. Toss it on a hot fire.'

Shane relinquished the bone. Clarry held it gingerly between two fingers as if he was about to catch the plague.

Blue growled.

Caddy watched as if trying to understand what everyone was on about.

Turning to leave, Clarry said, 'Where'd yer father get the dog? Don't want a dog bringin' old bones home. Or rubbishin' in carcasses she finds in the bush.'

Shrugging, Shane looked from Clarry to Caddy.

'Reckon you should tie her up,' Clarry said. 'Discourage her from that sort of thing. Wouldn't want her getting into anyone's livestock.'

To Shane, Caddy didn't seem like a dog that attacked livestock but he would tie her up, for a while at least, if it meant a bit of peace from Mr Johnson. He nodded.

Halfway to the van he turned to check on Clarry. He was almost halfway up his hill. He was hurrying like a man who could hear a distant phone ringing.

Strange guy, mused Shane.

Chapter 16
The End of the Day

Shane's father returned early. The afternoon sun was still high above the distant hills. He had some more sausages, a loaf of fresh bread and some potatoes. He also had a large bottle of Coke and several packets of crisps. He pushed them at Shane.

'Wrap yourself around some of that while I get the fire going. Reckon we might have a change tonight. We'll have a few spuds with our barbecued sausages!'

The Coke was still cold. Shane drank. He relaxed.

'Old Clarry was about again today. Reckon he can't keep away from the place. Sometimes he gives me the creeps,' added Shane idly.

'Yeah? How, this time?' inquired his father, looking up from his efforts to get the campfire going.

Shane explained how Old Clarry wanted to know what the police had said and how he was all stressed out about Caddy's find of an old wallaby bone.

Shane's father listened intently. 'Hmmm,' was his only comment.

Later, as they finished their crusty sausages, Shane said, 'Told me I should tie Caddy up. Wanted to know where you got Caddy? Seemed real interested in that.'

'None of the old busybody's business,' commented Shane's father softly. And when Shane looked up, his father was staring across the old paddock towards Clarry's shack.

'Reckons wallabies carry diseases,' continued Shane.

His father snorted his doubt.

'Finish your snag and let the poor dog off. Clarry will just have to live with the dog roaming free!'

Shane let Caddy off. She bounded around the van and was pleased with the discarded crusts Shane tossed her. His father shook his head with disapproval — but his eyes were smiling.

When Caddy wandered off, Shane's father told him about his afternoon. The police had taken a statement from him. They seemed more interested than he would have expected. The local newspaper had rung him. They were trying to make a big story out of the fire.

'I can just imagine the headlines,' he said, laughing. 'Mysterious Stranger Dies in Suspicious Fire! Police Make Further Inquiries.'

He stopped suddenly and listened. 'What's Caddy doing now?' He stood up and peered through the dusk.

Standing up, Shane could see Caddy digging at the ground at the edge of the slab of concrete.

'What's she after?' asked Shane's father. He didn't expect an answer.

'She was at that earlier in the day. Clarry put the stuff down. Going to build a shed or something. Caddy was sniffing around the edge.'

'Strange,' said his father quietly. He was silent for a moment. 'Still, we don't want Caddy turning the land into something that looks any more like a battle scene than it already does.' Whistling, he summoned Caddy. She looked up from her digging, waited a moment before rambling back to the campsite. 'Good girl,' he said as she settled down in the dirt near the campfire.

They sat in silence watching the dying fire, letting night spread her blanket of darkness. The bush birds were silent. A few scattered crickets made a desperate effort to crush the silence.

'Been a long day,' commented his father unexpectedly. 'It's amazing how such an event drains it out of you. Guess it's the stress and the talk, rather than the action. A bit different being on the other side of the desk. Might have to talk to the police again tomorrow. They expect forensic results fairly quickly.'

Silence.

Caddy's ears pricked. She growled softly, looking towards the dim light on the hill.

Clarry's dogs had a barking fit.

A moment later there was a shotgun blast.

The dogs went quiet.

'Bit drastic,' said Shane's father pouting his lip. 'Not real legal-like, either.'

Caddy watched the darkness.

Shane waited, not knowing what to expect next.

The dogs started barking again.

'Well, that didn't help much,' said Shane's father, stating the obvious.

'Maybe he's not a very good shot,' Shane offered.

'Wouldn't risk it,' advised his father.

The dogs went quiet. Silence. Bush silence.

Eventually Shane's father yawned, stood up and stretched. 'Think we'll call it a day. Might do some reading. Listen for our mysterious recorder player.' He looked at Shane across the dying embers.

Shane didn't react.

'Joke,' his father added, and walked around the campfire and rubbed Shane's head.

Shane at first tensed, but the mysterious music seemed a long way away. Just a little unreal. 'It seemed real at the time,' he said as he relaxed. He shrugged.

'Might just tie Caddy up to the steps of the van, all the same. Don't want another incident like last night.'

The thought made Shane shiver. Suddenly the bush darkness seemed more sinister. Less friendly. Closing in. He could imagine eyes in the night watching him.

And his father seemed to be more cautious than usual. Maybe his father wasn't telling him everything.

As they entered the van, Clarry's dogs started barking again.

Chapter 17
Another New Day

Before he left for work the next morning Shane's father said, 'Might leave you the mobile phone. I'd feel better if I could keep in contact.' He shrugged, then added, 'Maybe you could give your mother a call.'

Shane found it a little odd that his father would relinquish his phone for the day. It was important to his business. But it could give a bit of contact with the real world. Just having it nearby seemed to provide some comfort.

Yet, deep down he felt uncomfortable. He had a nagging fear that there were things happening that he wasn't aware of. The death of someone so close to where he had been sleeping was a gruesome thought.

Shane let Caddy off her lead. As he did so, he looked up to the shack on the hill. He caught a glimpse of 'Old Clarry' hurrying down his track to the road.

What's he up to now, wondered Shane.

Shane decided to make himself scarce, just in case Clarry decided to pay an unwelcome visit. He didn't want to talk to Clarry. It was hard enough at the best of times.

Calling Caddy, he headed for the boundary fence on the opposite side to Clarry's fence. The bush here was less degraded. The property on the other side of the fence was well-kept grazing land. A small herd of cattle grazed lazily on a small rise. Sturdy gums dotted the land.

Compared to Clarry's plot the farm was well managed. It was a scene that Shane found relaxing. He could imagine it on a calendar.

Unfortunately he didn't hear the mobile phone ringing in the van.

He wandered back towards the van as if he were on annual holidays.

His calm was soon shattered.

It might have been that for the briefest of moments he had caught it out of the corner of his eye. So brief that he ignored it.

It might have been the sudden change in Caddy's behaviour. One moment she was ambling along beside his legs, then she was alert, tense. She hadn't changed her pace but Shane sensed the change. He couldn't ignore the sudden feeling of alarm that flooded his body.

'Easy, girl,' he commanded as his eye searched the area from the van to the road.

Alert, Caddy obeyed. She growled quietly.

Then both Shane and Caddy stopped and watched Clarry. He was making his way around the burnt-out school.

He was closely inspecting the black mass of corrugated iron and charred beams.

He was carrying his old rifle.

When he reached the point where the body had been found he ducked under the chequered police tape and stood looking down to where the police had made their grim discovery. He kicked at the ashes with the toe of his boot.

'Steady, girl,' whispered Shane. He was tense and he could hear the blood throbbing through his temples.

Clarry looked up suspiciously, guiltily. He looked at the van, then as he surveyed the scene he caught sight of Shane and Caddy.

Shane sensed a fleeting moment of menace, annoyance, before Clarry stepped away from the ashes, ducked back under the tape and smiled. The smile was pasted on. Shane experienced a moment of revulsion.

Blue was sitting a little way off, in the shade, at the side of the road.

'OK, girl,' Shane muttered. He ushered Caddy back to her resting place behind the van with a quick, private flick of his wrist. She looked up at him and then trotted off. She looked back at Shane only once.

Clarry waved with his free hand.

Shane made his way across to Clarry. With his teeth clenched and his jaw beginning to ache he managed a thin smile.

'Shouldn't go in there,' he said to Clarry, a little more bluntly than he had hoped.

'Who'll know?' There was an edge of intimidation in Clarry's voice. 'Thought I might find somethin' the cops missed.' He smiled, almost sweetly. He started following the tape around the perimeter of the building remains, as if to prove his point.

Not likely, thought Shane. Reluctantly, he followed Clarry to the back of the burnt-out building. He couldn't see if Caddy was still waiting near the van. Glancing over his shoulder he saw Blue looking back down the road.

He almost bumped into Clarry, who had suddenly stopped. He had a vivid picture of Clarry's back and of Clarry's clenched hands. He was slowly flexing his fingers.

'Oops!' Shane squawked, feeling silly.

Clarry didn't move. He was looking at the places where Caddy had been digging at the edges of the slab.

'What's she doing that for?' Shane took a moment to comprehend Clarry's snarled question.

Shane was about to bumble about for an answer when he realised he was not obliged to answer Clarry's rather rude questions. It wasn't his property any more. He didn't have to defend what his dog did.

Clarry turned around and Shane stepped back. He could see the threat and anger in Clarry's eyes.

Finding his voice, Shane made an effort to reply.

'She's just … just doing what dogs do.' He shrugged to show it wasn't important. His confidence slowly returned. 'It doesn't matter anyway! Dad's going to get rid of that concrete slab when he starts our farm.'

'Ain't farming country!' snapped Clarry. 'Dog'll end up digging holes anywhere.'

What's it matter, Shane thought. He couldn't understand Clarry's intense hostility. And he was having trouble hiding his disdain for Clarry's intrusion. His heart was beating rapidly. He was not in control of the situation and he wondered why he felt defensive. He was beginning to feel angry.

'Dog'll end up getting hurt,' Clarry said slowly, deliberately.

Shane shook his head, bewildered by the statement.

'Mark my words, son.' Clarry fondled his rifle.

For an eternity neither person spoke. Clarry seemed to be waiting for Shane to concur; Shane not knowing how to react.

'City folk don't understand how things are done in the bush.' There was a warning in Clarry's voice.

Shane was out of his depth. It was a situation he didn't understand. Suddenly, to his relief, Caddy was by his side. He rubbed her head with his hand without taking his eyes off Clarry.

He watched as Clarry visibly tensed.

On the roadside Blue barked. When Shane cast his eyes in that direction he could see Blue was not interested in his and Clarry's stand-off. Blue's attention was drawn to something down the road.

Shane's alarm and confusion moved up a notch.

Chapter 18
Escalation!

Blue's interest was in Ellie, as she dreamily pushed her pram up the centre of the rutted road.

Clarry's interest was on Caddy.

It took Shane a moment to realise that Clarry was momentarily stranded in a state somewhere between disbelief and fury. His eyes were wide and his mouth was open. Shane could see the irregular, broken line of teeth.

Caddy sensed his fear. She growled ominously.

Clarry snapped out of his trance. 'Bloody dog!' he hissed.

Looking at Caddy, Shane saw the reason for Clarry's fury. His vehemence was about to explode. Any moment Shane feared he would become a raving idiot. And all Caddy had was a few more small bones!

Blue started to bark, but Clarry was transfixed by Caddy's changing posture. She was tense and the hairs on the back of her neck stood up. She growled threateningly through her closed mouth.

Foolishly, Clarry put his hand out to take Caddy's find.

Caddy dropped the bundle of bones and snapped at Clarry's outstretched hand. She moved forward.

Clarry stepped back, gasping, but his eyes were fixed on Caddy's. He made a move to defend himself with his rifle. It was a red rag to Caddy. Immediately, she was ready to spring.

'Caddy!' cried Shane. His voice almost cracked.

In the distance, Blue barked twice.

Clarry recognised his mistake. He stepped back and carefully lowered his rifle. He glared at Shane.

Caddy held her attack pose. She snarled menacingly.

Clarry shuffled back, getting more distance between himself and the dog. Suddenly, he looked like a snivelling coward.

'Caddy,' said Shane. Back off, he was warning.

Clarry continued to shuffle back, hardly moving his feet. His pretence of indifference would have been comical if the situation hadn't been so tense, unreal. He hit the edge of the concrete slab. Slowly, he did a backwards step onto it.

'That dog's a bloody menace!' Clarry hissed, hardly moving his lips.

Shane found his voice. 'They're only more wallaby bones!' he maintained. 'What's the big deal?'

'Don't be a smartass! You don't know nothing.'

Caddy, who had begun to relax, was immediately defensive.

Clarry looked around nervously. It was then he realised he had an audience. Ellie and Blue.

'What are you watchin'?' he yelled, forgetting Caddy for a moment. With sudden realisation of his error his head jerked back to see what the dog was doing.

Caddy hadn't moved but she was tense.

Visibly relaxing, Clarry returned his attention to Ellie. 'Well?' he thundered.

Ellie was confused — and visibly hurt. Her face dropped.

'Lost yer tongue, young lady? Take yerself home.'

Ellie was too upset to move. Or too frightened. Her inaction was disobedience to the enraged Clarry. After another contemptuous glance in Caddy's direction, Clarry strode off across the grounds to the gap in the front fence that was once the front gate.

'Get going!' ordered Clarry with a wild impatient sweep of his arm. Ellie didn't have the presence of mind to move. She was riveted to a spot in the middle of the road, unable to make any decision.

In utter frustration Clarry grabbed at the old cane pram in an angry attempt to turn it back toward his place.

Its worn wheels, caught in the gravel, didn't roll. The pram tumbled over, spilling its contents.

Ellie screamed, suddenly no longer transfixed by the scene she had been witnessing. She rushed forward to grab the doll that now lay in a crumpled heap. Madly she scrambled about, almost on hands and knees, gathering her possessions. A pillow. A small plastic toy. A blanket. A thin dirty mattress.

And all the time, as she scrambled about she held her doll protectively against her chest.

Then she stood up, pulling the pram back onto its wheels. She glared at Clarry. Clarry just shook his head with contempt.

'Get rid of the bloody thing, you fool! It's only a bloody doll,' he snapped. 'You treat it as if it's a real kid! Grow up!'

Ellie's eyes narrowed. She didn't move.

Unable to contain his frustration a moment longer, Clarry grabbed at the pram and gave it a mighty push towards the side of the road. It bounced and rocked over the corrugations, not tipping over until it rolled clumsily into the dry gutter.

A vehicle was grinding its way down the road. Clarry looked around.

Suddenly Ellie was beating her father with a clenched fist. She was screaming accusations at him, all the time shielding her doll from the violence.

For a moment Clarry tried to fend her off with his free hand. Then, in an act of sheer spite, he snatched Ellie's doll and flung it along the road.

The car honked. Ellie and her father separated, as if by some predetermined agreement, to opposite sides of the road as the car passed between them.

It was the mail car. The driver slowed, took his hands off the wheel for a moment and raised them with a shrug. He wasn't about to stop.

As he picked up speed he honked again. But he took no notice of the doll lying in the gravel.

Ellie screamed as if she had been possessed by devils. She stared in grief and disbelief at the smashed doll, lying flattened in the middle of the road.

Blue growled and barked, confused.

Clarry took his rifle in two hands and marched off. 'Get home!' he yelled at Ellie, but didn't look back. Blue took off after him.

Ellie watched him for a moment. Then she yelled at his back, 'You can't keep doing this. That's how you solve everything. You spoil everything. You can't stand to see anyone else happy! I'm not doing anything you say! You're an animal. Animal! Animal!'

Suddenly Ellie stopped. She looked towards the house on the hill. She had determined on a course of action. She skirted the broken doll, avoiding looking directly at it. She left the road and clambered through the fence and up through Clarry's old orchard to the shanty.

Shane could see her nearing the shanty, well before Clarry was halfway up his long drive. The dogs started barking.

He shook his head and squatted down next to Caddy, visibly shaken by the whole sequence of events. He absently touched the bones that Caddy had dropped, played with them with his index finger. His finger touched something other than bone. He peered at the little heap of small bones, thinking they were probably the bones of a wallaby's foot.

He cautiously isolated something circular. He pushed it away from the blackened bones, rubbing it carefully across the surface of the concrete. He didn't like what he was discovering.

Gingerly, he picked up his find. He turned it over. It was metal and the sun glinted on its shiny gold surface where it had been rubbed against the concrete.

It was a ring. Not unlike a wedding ring.

Chapter 19
Sinister Developments

Shane stood shakily. He didn't like what he was thinking. There was a body in the bush! There was a tightness in his chest and his legs felt weak. Forcing himself to walk he made his way across to the van, his eyes on the bush behind it, wondering what gruesome secret it held.

He pushed open the door. 'Sit, Caddy,' he ordered. The last thing he wanted was Caddy rushing back into the bush and bringing back another hand, or foot … or skull.

Two bodies in two days. He shook his head in disbelief, but his disbelief was giving way to fear.

He found the mobile phone and punched in his father's work number. He was shaking nervously.

It was answered by the receptionist. Shane asked to talk to his father.

He was told that his father could not be contacted immediately but she could give him a message.

'Tell him Shane rang,' he said, not sure how much to pass on over the phone.

He dropped the phone on his father's bed. Unsure, unable to think logically.

Who was buried in the bush?

He remembered Clarry. His strange behaviour. Clarry had always been odd, but maybe, just maybe, Clarry was not merely a nosy busybody neighbour.

Shane's blood ran cold. It was as if he had been given a jigsaw and didn't know what the picture was, concealed in the mess of pieces. Now he had accidentally joined several of the bits. And the picture he was getting was strange, but incomplete.

A vehicle honked out on the road. Startled, Shane looked nervously out the window. He was getting panicky. He didn't know what to expect.

It was the mail car on its return run. A feeling of relief surged through Shane's body.

The driver honked again. Shane dashed out the door and hurried to the front gate. Caddy trotted after him.

The mailman leaned out of the car window. He was waving a rolled-up paper.

'Thought you might like to see this, it's the local rag. You get a mention,' called the driver. 'Didn't like to drop it on the way through with Old Clarry arguing in the middle of the road.'

Shane took the paper with thanks.

'I'd watch that guy. He's a bit odd. What do you think of Ellie?' He was smiling. 'Nasty business that,' he nodded to the burnt-out school.

Shane wasn't sure how to answer. He didn't want to think about Clarry.

The driver eased back onto the road. 'Drop you a paper each week now that I know someone's here. It will help to fill in your time — at least five minutes of it!' He laughed and disappeared in a cloud of dust, giving one final blast of the horn.

It was a thin paper — no more than sixteen pages. Shane quickly thumbed through it as he made his way back to the van. The ink had bled from one side of the page to the next and there was an overuse of red, the only colour, in an attempt to brighten it up.

At first, he didn't find any article on the school fire. Plenty of articles on sport and pictures of councillors. He went back to the front page. He found it, though it took a moment to see the connection between the headline and the report.

SCHOOL NOT TO REOPEN AFTER TRAGEDY

LATE on the night of Tuesday 15 January the school at Ironbark Ridge was burnt to the ground. Opened in 1887 this school provided education for the students of the small community of Ironbark Ridge for over 100 years until it was closed by the previous government. Community efforts to have it reopened have been unsuccessful.

The fire that destroyed the school was well alight when the Ironbark Ridge Bushfire Brigade arrived. It was impossible to save it, said Fire Captain Les Murphy.

Police were called to the scene when firemen became suspicious when informed that the building may have been 'occupied'.

Police found the body of what is believed to be an itinerant worker. When questioned, a police spokesperson said they didn't know the identity of the victim. They were, however, continuing their investigation and couldn't rule out foul play at this stage. It is understood that foul play is not ruled out until after police receive the coroner's report.

Mr David Goodman, who recently bought the old school block, said that the fire may have been started by a dropped cigarette. There had been evidence that the old building was being used as a shelter by swaggies. Mr Goodman said that the police want to speak to him again.

Mr Goodman hopes to grow grapes and olives on the land.

As he made his way back to the van Shane became aware of the phone ringing in the van.

It was his father. He spoke with urgency. He told Shane he had spoken to the police a second time. It would appear that the fire victim had met his death in suspicious circumstances. His skull had been smashed with a blunt instrument — probably a piece of wood.

Shane was silent.

'Listen,' said his father, 'I want you to be very careful. This is not public knowledge, but police are convinced the guy was murdered. Worries me that there's some sort of maniac wandering around out there. I hate to think about it. Keep Caddy with you all the time.'

'Dad,' said Shane quietly, 'there's something else.'

His father was immediately suspicious. 'Yes?'

In disjointed sentences, Shane reported what had happened during the morning. He could almost sense his father's silent alarm over the phone.

For a moment the line started to break up.

'Stay near the van. We've got a problem but we'll be OK if we keep our heads. Keep the phone with you all the time and if anyone comes onto the property, anyone, phone the police on the emergency number. I'm going to call them now. Stay tight. Don't let Caddy wander off. She's a good dog. Well trained, thank God!'

The phone started to crackle. 'I should be home shortly. I'm actually on my way. I've just passed through ...' The message was lost. 'I've got a company phone ... the number ...' More static and crackle.

'Dad!' called Shane, as if talking louder would help the deteriorating connection. The next few words his father spoke were unintelligible.

'Dad, I can't hear you! Dad!'

The phone went dead in Shane's hand. He looked at it, waiting for it to ring again. With a sinking feeling he realised it wasn't going to. He didn't know what to do. He paced the length of the van, his nerves taut. There was an ache in the pit of his stomach. He paced back the other way. Events over which he had no control were crowding in on him.

He had no plan except to wait for his father — and hope nothing happened.

He looked out the small kitchen window across the burnt-out school. He wished he had never seen the place.

Clarry was standing on the road. His gun hung by his side. He looked like a man with a mission.

Shane felt sick.

Chapter 20

The Hunter and the Hunted

Clarry walked to the front gate. He stood, sullen, eyes fixed on the van.

Shane lowered his body cautiously, half expecting Clarry to have X-ray vision. He peered out over the window ledge, keeping to one side of the small cafe curtain. Clarry hadn't moved. Shane felt vulnerable.

Outside, Caddy growled.

'Quiet, girl!' Shane hissed.

Clarry advanced into the school grounds. The rifle now pointed at the ground several metres in front of where he was slowly walking. He looked as if he was stalking a wild beast.

Caddy growled again. Again Shane hissed his command. But the intrusion and the feeling of threat were too much for her.

Shane remembered the phone. He grabbed it from his father's bed. He fumbled with the buttons, his fingers trembling. Looking over his shoulder he could see Clarry still advancing on the van. But his eyes were fixed on Caddy. Caddy had moved to place herself between Clarry and the van. She was out in the open!

Smiling, Clarry raised the barrel of the gun just a little higher.

Caddy growled. She lowered her body into an attack position.

'Just try it, mutt!' Clarry threatened.

The emergency number answered with a warning about the misuse of emergency numbers.

Clarry was playing with his rifle, taunting Caddy to react. She held her position. Clarry moved a small, deliberate step forward, testing her resolve. He was keeping a safe distance.

'Name?' said the voice on the phone.

Shane blurted out his name and everything that seemed important. He was almost incoherent, his voice trembled. He watched Clarry move another step towards Caddy and the van. Now he held the rifle ready to shoot. One hand held the barrel, the other was cupping the trigger mechanism.

'Come on, dog!' Clarry snarled.

'I'm going to kill that dog!' he shouted at the world in general.

On the phone: 'Slow down and answer the questions. We'll need the facts if we are to help.' The voice was reassuring, confident.

Shane answered the questions, watching the slow-motion tableau in the schoolyard.

Caddy was tense, ready to spring — but Clarry was not within range.

He raised the rifle. 'One dead dog,' he said with relish. Shane dropped the phone and rushed to the door. As he tumbled through the narrow opening he screamed, 'Caddy!' The van swayed. Clarry's attention was diverted for a moment.

As Shane swung around the front of the van Caddy was rushing Clarry. Clarry realised his mistake, but he was too experienced a hunter to lose control in a sudden change of circumstance. He whipped the gun up to his shoulder and aimed at the advancing dog.

Shane screamed again as a shot thundered out. The next few moments were turmoil in Shane's mind. The first shot was followed by a sharper rifle crack and a bullet went through the side of the van.

Clarry was grabbing at his bloodied face. He had dropped the rifle and Caddy was on top of him, bringing him to the ground. He yelled in pain and anger.

Shane stood transfixed. The events didn't fit together. Clarry lay huddled on the ground protecting his head and groaning loudly. Caddy growled menacingly at his throat.

From behind some bushes emerged Ellie. She held a double-barrelled shotgun and was advancing on Clarry. Her jaw was set and her eyes were fixed on her victim.

Caddy eyed her suspiciously, swaying slightly. Ready.

'Bastard!' Ellie said as she advanced.

It dawned upon Shane with frightening simplicity that she was going to blast her father.

'Don't!' gasped Shane. Ellie looked at him as if he didn't exist.

A vehicle roared into the grounds, horn blaring.

It rushed up to where Clarry lay on the ground, stopping just a metre or so from his body. Caddy moved back.

For a brief second Shane thought his father was going to run over Clarry.

In the distance he could hear a siren, getting louder. Then it was all over.

As Shane crumpled, his father was by his side holding him, speaking to him, reassuring him.

Shane was only vaguely aware of the police car, lights flashing, screaming to a halt next to his father's ute. He vaguely remembered an ambulance.

He dimly remembered Ellie standing, all alone, watching the events unfolding before her. He felt a pang of sadness, regret that he couldn't explain.

Aftermath

Clarry was taken away in an ambulance, under police guard. Shane saw that much, but the full story took time to be revealed. Even his father didn't know all the facts.

Shane's father had got Caddy from the police. She was a sniffer dog that had been pensioned off. It had been thought that a retirement in the bush would be appropriate — a nice reward for Caddy's years of service. No one had imagined the crimes Clarry had committed — and Caddy hadn't earned her reputation sniffing for drugs at airports but sniffing for bodies. Cadavers, as the police called them.

More pieces of Shane's jigsaw were falling into place.

The next week the local paper filled in more details.

GRIM FIND IN THE BUSH
Man Charged with Multiple Murders

DEVELOPMENTS at Ironbark Ridge took a shocking turn last week. A number of mysterious disappearances from the district over the last few years have been cleared up.

A police spokesperson has told the 'Rural Voice' that they had been watching Clarry Johnson for some time. Clarry Johnson has been charged with the murder of Geoff Bowls. Bowls had been clubbed over the head, in the old Ironbark Ridge School, before the school had been set alight. Johnson has also been charged with arson.

Johnson has also been charged with the murder of his wife. Her body was found in a shallow grave behind the Ironbark Ridge School. Initial reports show that her skull was smashed and she had been shot.

The body of a small baby was found buried under a slab of concrete in the Ironbark Ridge School grounds. Johnson has been charged with the murder of an unnamed infant. Police are continuing their questioning of Johnson in regard to a number of other disappearances in the area.

Police have grave concerns for Ellie Johnson who has not been seen since the incident. Information on her whereabouts is sought.

Police admit that their investigations have been helped by an ex-police dog which has made some grim finds.

And so the report went on, explaining, describing and sensationalising.

Shane's father had hooked the caravan up to the ute.

'It was a great dream, but we couldn't stay here,' he said as they sat around their last campfire, 'always wondering what we might find every time we planted a tree, or dug a hole.'

A weak breeze had sprung up.

Shane tossed Caddy a crust. He looked towards Clarry Johnson's place and involuntarily shuddered.

Then he looked in the other direction, across the paddocks. The sun was slipping towards the distant mountains. Cattle were grazing near the fence. The scene was serene and relaxing. He sighed deeply. He was missing company, his kind of company.

Then he heard it. Three melancholy, rising notes in a minor key.

Wide-eyed, Shane looked at his father. His father, forehead creased, looked around. Everything seemed in place. The dog hadn't stirred.

Memories of the nightmare night came flooding back to Shane.

The breeze stirred the campfire ashes.

The three notes were repeated. They came from somewhere near the van. Caddy ignored them.

Shane's father stood up and walked purposefully to the side of the van. But his face still showed bewilderment. He shook his head. In mock heroics he even looked under the van. As he did so the notes sounded again.

He stood up and smiled. 'Your phantom flute player,' he announced, his open hand pointing to the side of the van. 'Just wait!'

As the gentle breeze picked up, the notes were played again.

'There's your culprit,' said Shane's father smugly. Shane stood up, not understanding.

'Just call me Sherlock. Might get a job with the local police! Noticed that we only heard the notes when the wind blew ever so gently. When the air crossed over the vents here,' he pointed to the vents at the back of the van's fridge. 'Must admit it did occur to me earlier, but …' he shrugged, then grinned. 'Only seems to happen when the breeze is coming at a certain speed and in a certain direction. Freak of nature.'

The last piece of the jigsaw had fallen into place.

The End

Alan Horsfield has written multiple school texts and over 30 children's stories for all age groups up to young adult. Some have been selected for state premiers' reading lists. Alan is the past President of the NSW Children's Book Council (CBC) and was a judge for the NSW (Children's) Book Awards.

Thank you for reading *Cadaver Dog*. Here are some of my recent books available as ebooks or in print directly from anehorsfield@westnet.com.au.

Check out: **alanhorsfield.com.au**

A wide range of school texts are available from Pascal Press (Excel) and Five Senses Education.

www.ingramcontent.com/pod-product-compliance
Lightning Source LLC
Chambersburg PA
CBHW070348120726
47909CB00008B/2765